# The Rootomom Tree

Meg Elbow

Illustrated by Lynn Munsinger

Houghton Mifflin Company Boston 1978

Library of Congress Cataloging in Publication Data

Elbow, Margaret B.
  The Rootomom Tree.

  SUMMARY: A young boy accepts the advice and
help of the jungle animals to rid himself of the
Rootomom Tree that has sprouted from his head.
  [1.  Animals — Fiction.  2.  Jungle stories]
I.  Munsinger, Lynne.  II.  Title.
PZ7.E356Ro    [E]       77-26696
ISBN 0-395-26452-9

# The Rootomom Tree

Benja darted into the hut where his mother was poking at the dying fire under a rice pot. He squatted beside her on the dirt floor.

"Mother, I'm hungry," he said. "When will the rice be ready?"

"When you bring me some dung to burn," his mother said. "Rice won't cook on cold ashes."

"I can't find anymore dung. It's all been gathered."

"Then you'll have to go to the forest and bring back some borra bark."

Benja clapped his hands.

"I like the forest. I like the animals there. And I can find seeds and berries to eat."

He skipped past his mother as she lifted the rice pot off the ashes.

"Wait, Benja! You've never been to the forest alone. If you find salapala seeds and birny berries you may eat them, but never, never eat the seed in the rootomom fruit. Off you go. And hurry back with the borra bark!" she called after him.

Benja ran to the forest. It was cool among the trees and he lingered over his task of collecting bark. After a while he spied a salapala tree. Its long, curling pods hung down bulging with seeds.

I'm as hungry as an elephant, he thought. I'll eat some salapala seeds.

He picked a handful of pods and sat on the great roots of the tree shelling out the seeds and eating them one by one. He ate so many seeds he grew thirsty.

Now I'll look for a birny bush. Birny berries are juicy, he said to himself.

Benja searched along the pathways of the forest but he could not find a birny bush. He was about to gather up his bark and go home when he caught his toe in a root and tripped and fell. There by his nose on the ground lay a round, ripe rootomom fruit. Clear, cool juice oozed from its core.

I'll drink the juice from this fruit, he thought. It will quench my thirst.

Benja picked up the fruit, tilted back his head, and opened his mouth. Fresh, sweet juice fell on his tongue. He squeezed with all his might. Out popped a seed and before Benja could stop it, the seed slid down his throat.

What have I done? thought Benja in alarm. Was that the seed from the rootomom fruit?

He stood up. An odd tingling spread from his toes to his head and made him dizzy. Reaching up with his hands, he could feel something parting his hair.

"What's happening to me?" he cried. Tears of fright rolled down his cheeks and splashed onto his dusty brown feet. Suddenly there was a squawk in his ear.

"I see you are in trouble, my young friend." Jara, the parrot, perched on a limb above Benja's head. "You swallowed the forbidden seed and from it will grow a tree. For a year and a day the tree will always be with you."

Benja sank down on the forest path. He could feel the rootomom tree sprouting from his head. It grew bigger all the time. The branches filled with leaves, which shook and rustled when he moved. One branch bent suddenly in front of Benja's face as Jara hopped onto it.

"Benja, there is only one way to rid yourself of the rootomom tree," Jara said. "When a year has passed your tree will bear a rootomom fruit. If you can persuade Kirak, the vulture, to eat the seed inside it your tree will die. The spell will then be broken. Heed what I say," said Jara, and flew off into the forest.

Benja started to rise but the tree on his head made him top-heavy. Slowly he stood upright. Above him the rootomom branches began to sway violently and he was afraid he would topple over. Then, through a cluster of leaves, two bright eyes peered down at him.

"Hello, Benja, I'm Momo," said a little monkey, who was looking into his face. "I would like to come and live in your tree."

"But I don't live in the forest. I came here to gather borra bark for my mother. How can I gather it now?"

Benja looked down in dismay at the borra bark lying at his feet.

"I'll help you, Benja," said Momo, "if I can live in your tree wherever you go."

He swung down from the tree and scampered about picking up borra bark. He brought it to Benja and filled his arms.

"You have as much bark as you can carry, Benja," said Momo.

"Let's take it home to your mother." He leaped back into the rootomom tree and perched above Benja's head.

Benja made his way slowly along the pathway out of the woods. Every time one of the rootomom branches caught on another tree the little monkey freed it. Soon they left the forest behind.

When Benja reached his hut, his mother was inside.

"Here's your bark, Mother," he called.

"Bring it in, Benja," she answered.

"I can't, Mother. I can't come in the door."

Then Benja's mother knew what had happened.

"Benja, Benja, you are cursed," she said, as she came out of the hut. "For the rest of your life you will carry the rootomom tree on your head."

"Jara told me it would only be for a year and a day."

"What else did Jara tell you?"

"He told me that at the end of a year and a day my tree would have a fruit, and if I could persuade Kirak to eat the seed in it, my tree would die."

"That's all very well, my son, but a flower comes before the fruit. How will you protect the flower from insects? If insects don't destroy it, how will you prevent the fruit from being eaten by birds? How will you persuade Kirak to swallow its seed?"

Benja hung his head.

"I hadn't thought of all that," he said, unhappily. He dropped the borra bark at his mother's feet. She picked it up and went into the hut.

Benja leaned on the wall of the hut. As he stood there, miserably scuffling his toes in the dust, he felt something tickle his neck. The tickle ran down his arm, over his wrist, and onto his hand. He blinked and saw a little green lizard sitting on his knuckles.

"I'm Chakeetoh," the lizard said. "If you'll let me live in your tree I'll watch over the flower as it grows. Before insects can harm it I'll catch them with a flick of my tongue."

"Thank you, Chakeetoh. You're my friend," Benja said. "I'm glad you want to live in my tree with Momo, the monkey."

Chakeetoh ran back up Benja's arm and over his head into the rootomom tree. He was soon hidden among the leaves.

Benja's mother came out of the hut with a bowl in her hand.

"The borra bark made a good fire. Here's your rice, Benja. Sit down and eat it."

Benja sat cross-legged on the ground. While he was eating his rice Chakeetoh ran down his arm and lay on the rim of his bowl, staring at him with glittering eyes. Momo played peek-a-boo in the leaves over his head.

"Mother, where will I sleep tonight?" Benja asked. "The hut's too small."

"You can lay your mat by the wall outside and sleep under your tree. I won't be far away."

Benja unrolled his sleeping mat. When he lay down, the leaves of the rootomom tree drooped around him. Somewhere in the branches over his head his new friends, the monkey and the lizard, were nestled for the night.

Benja was awakened in the morning by a rustling and a chattering in the rootomom tree.

"Time to get up, Benja," chattered Momo. "Time to get up."

Benja stretched and the leaves of the rootomom tree uncurled from around him. Its branches straightened above him. Carefully he sat up. He looked at the rising sun and its glowing orb reminded him of the shiny, orange rootomom fruit whose juice he had drunk the day before.

So much has happened since yesterday, Benja thought. If only I hadn't swallowed the rootomom seed.

"Mother," he said, as his mother appeared with his bowl of rice, "you told me that I must protect the rootomom fruit and I must persuade Kirak to eat its seed. How can I do these things?"

"That's for you to find out, my son. I cannot help you. Hurry and eat your rice. Since you cannot stoop to gather dung, you must go each day to the forest for borra bark."

As Benja was finishing his rice, Chakeetoh slid down his arm and lay on the rim of his bowl as before.

"Benja," he whispered, "I've discovered a bud on your rootomom tree. I'll guard it so the flower will grow safely." He ran back into the tree.

"Momo! Chakeetoh! It's time to go for borra bark," said Benja.

Slowly he stood erect. Momo swung from the lowest branches of the rootomom tree and made faces at Benja as he walked toward the forest.

"When we reach the forest, let's ask the weaver birds to make some baskets to hang from my tree," he said to Momo. "Then we can fill them with borra bark and take more home to my mother."

They came to the thick forest. Benja threaded his way among the trees, the monkey disentangling the rootomom branches when they caught on other limbs. At a place where borra bark was plentiful Benja stopped and Momo ran about collecting it and piling it at his feet. Benja was so busy watching him that he was surprised by a raucous voice in his ear.

"Good morning, Benja," squawked Jara. "How did you sleep? How are you and your tree?"

"The tree is heavy," said Benja. "I wish the year and a day were over. How can I be sure the flower will bloom? How do I know the fruit will ripen? How can I persuade Kirak to eat its seed? Where can I find some weaver birds to make baskets to carry bark home to my mother?"

"One thing at a time, my young friend, one thing at a time! The flower and fruit will grow at their own pace. But baskets for bark would be useful now. I'll summon the weaver birds." With a flap of his green and red wings Jara was gone.

Soon a twittering and a fluttering told Benja that the weaver birds had arrived. He watched them as they flitted in and out among the shadowy tree trunks and the swinging yanghi vines. With their beaks they cut the vines and deftly wove them around the lowest branches of the rootomom tree. Gradually, pointed

nestlike baskets took shape and hung down around Benja. Glee-fully, Momo picked up the bark at Benja's feet and filled the baskets.

"My mother will be happy to have so much borra bark," Benja said. "Skillful weaver birds, how can I thank you?"

"You can break open some salapala pods and give us their seeds," twittered the weaver birds. "We like them as much as you do."

Quickly Benja gathered handfuls of salapala pods and broke them open and scattered the seeds on the ground. The weaver birds fluttered about his feet, pecking up the seeds as rapidly as they had woven the baskets. Soon every seed had disappeared.

"I'll shell salapala seeds for you every day if you'll come for them," Benja said.

"A salapala feast once in a while is enough," twittered the weaver birds, and with a dip of their long tails they fluttered away into the dim green depths of the forest.

Momo jumped onto the edge of one of the weaver birds' baskets and set it swinging.

"D'you think we have enough bark for today, Benja?" he asked.

"More than enough," Benja said. "Let's go home."

He set off for the village, almost hidden by the baskets filled with bark swinging around him.

Benja's mother was delighted to have plenty of borra bark for her fire. Sometimes she sold what she did not need and then there would be a little meat mixed with the rice in Benja's bowl.

Every night as Benja ate his rice Chakeetoh rested on the rim of his bowl. And every night Chakeetoh told him about the bud on the rootomom tree which was opening little by little. Then one night Chakeetoh said: "Today the bud burst into flower."

"I wish I could see it," Benja said. "Tell me about it."

"The flower is beautiful. It has a pale purple trumpet with a dark purple fringe lining its throat. A powdery, yellow tongue curls from its center. At the back of the tongue is the beginning of the rootomom fruit."

"We must guard it night and day, Chakeetoh."

"Soon I won't be much help, Benja. The flower will die after ZuZuZ, the bee, has brought pollen to it. It'll drop off and soon the fruit will grow. Birds may attack the fruit, and birds are my enemies too."

"Tomorrow when we go to the forest we must ask Jara what to do," said Benja.

Next day in the forest Benja waited and watched for Jara. Momo finished gathering borra bark and began jumping impatiently on and off the baskets. Benja began to worry that Jara was not coming. He was about to start back to the village when Jara flapped down with a squawk and curled his claws around a rootomom branch.

"So your tree has flowered, Benja. The fruit will come next. It's time to send for the popping toads."

"Why do I need popping toads?"

"To protect the rootomom fruit. Don't you know how popping toads sound?"

"I've never heard them," said Benja.

"Then it's time you did. As popping toads croak, their cheeks blow into enormous bubbles which collapse with a mighty bang. The noise is enough to scare away a flock of birds. It'll make you jump too, if you're not expecting it," chuckled Jara as he flew away.

Benja walked home, smiling at Momo's antics. Momo was leap-
ing from basket to basket of borra bark, making them swing
wildly. When they were out of the forest and halfway across the
plain, Momo cried: "Look, Benja! Here comes ZuZuZ!"

Flying slowly, because she was laden with pollen, ZuZuZ ap-
proached Benja.

"My pollen baskets are heavy," she buzzed. "Where's your rootomom flower to empty them into?"

"Above my head," said Benja. "Chakeetoh will show you. Chakeetoh!"

In a green flash, Chakeetoh slid out of the tree and sat on Benja's ear.

"Follow me, ZuZuZ," he said.

ZuZuZ disappeared behind Chakeetoh as he slithered back among the rootomom leaves. Soon ZuZuZ flew out of the tree.

"Your tree will bear a perfect rootomom fruit," she buzzed at Benja. "From now on, watch your step lest you trip and shake the fruit off before it's ripe." With a whirring of her wings she buzzed away.

When Benja went for bark next day, he was met by a band of popping toads. In the quiet of the forest the noise of the toads was startling.

"So you're the popping toads," Benja exclaimed. "What a racket you make!"

"Jara said you needed us to frighten bird thieves from your rootomom tree," croaked the toads.

"I do. The fruit growing on my tree must be protected. Chakee-toh kept insects from the flower but the fruit is in danger from birds. Will you hop into my tree?"

"Squat down then," said a grandfather toad. "We can't reach your tree in one jump."

Cautiously Benja squatted down. He blinked as the toads leaped from his feet to his knees to his shoulders to his head and into the rootomom tree. Once they were lost among the leaves they were silent.

"Popping toads," called Benja, "why don't you croak?"

"We've shown you our secret," said the grandfather toad. "If we croaked all the time our noise wouldn't scare the birds."

"You're right," said Benja. "I hadn't thought of that."

Benja rose to his feet. The empty weaver birds' baskets swayed gently as he moved.

"Momo, where are you? It's time to fill the baskets."

"Here I am, Benja," said the little monkey, creeping out from behind a big tree trunk. "I was hiding from the popping toads."

"If they frighten you then they'll surely frighten the birds," laughed Benja. "The rootomom fruit will be safe."

When the baskets were full of borra bark Benja and his friends left the forest. A hawk was circling over the plain. Slowly it began descending toward the rootomom tree. As it was stretching its legs to alight, the popping toads croaked. The tree exploded with sound and the hawk wheeled upward in fright.

"Popping toads, you terrified that bird," said Benja. "It will never come back."

The days went by and the rootomom fruit kept on growing. From a hard green beginning it swelled into a juicy, orange fruit. At last the fruit reached perfection. It was as round and shiny and orange and juicy as it would ever be.

"The rootomom fruit is ripe now, Benja." Chakeetoh slid out from his hiding place in the leaves. "It's getting ready to fall from the tree."

"We must ask Jara's advice again. Tomorrow we'll tell him the fruit is ripe."

Next day when Benja and his friends reached the forest, Jara was waiting.

"So you need me again," he said, fluttering his wings as he swayed back and forth on a branch in front of Benja.

"Chakeetoh says the rootomom fruit is ripe," Benja said. "How can I persuade Kirak to swallow its seed?"

"That," said Jara, "is the hardest challenge. You know that vultures eat dead flesh. But if they're really hungry they will eat

fruit. I've seen to it that Kirak is starving. I called the jackals from far and wide to hunt in all of Kirak's haunts and they haven't left a shred of meat for him to eat. If we can lure him to your rootomom fruit I expect he will devour it."

"Do you know a way?" asked Benja.

"We'll need help from the carpenter ants and Pengli Possum. We'll ask the carpenter ants to saw off all the leaves that hide the rootomom fruit."

"But even if he can see it, what will make Kirak decide to eat it?"

"That's why we need Pengli Possum. She knows how to pretend she is dead well enough to fool even a vulture."

"But I don't want Kirak to eat Pengli," protested Benja. "Besides, if Kirak ate Pengli, he wouldn't want my rootomom fruit."

"You're right, my young friend, but Pengli won't be eaten. She's too clever for Kirak. Kirak won't eat anything alive and Pengli will only *play* dead beside the rootomom fruit. In the end Kirak will be so hungry he will eat it. Now let me find Pengli and the carpenter ants."

Soon an army of ants appeared, marching along the path to Benja's feet. They swarmed up his bare legs and under his shirt. They came out at his neck and marched over his head into the rootomom tree.

"Please wait till we're on the plain before you begin sawing off the rootomom leaves," Benja said to the ants. "I want to be where Kirak can see me."

"Don't worry," said the ants. "We'll wait for your signal."

"The bark's all gathered, Benja." Momo swung from a yanghi vine and landed with a thump at Benja's feet.

"We can't leave the forest until Pengli comes," Benja said.

"Perhaps Jara couldn't find her." Momo peered into the treetops. "What's that, Benja?"

Leaves danced on a tree in front of them.

"You wanted me, Benja?" said the soft voice of Pengli Possum. Her pointed nose poked through the leaves. "Jara sent me. He said you needed someone to play dead for Kirak. Can anyone do that better than I?"

"No one," said Benja. "Climb into my tree and join my friends. Somewhere carpenter ants, popping toads, and Chakeetoh are hiding. Be careful not to shake down the rootomom fruit."

"If I choose, I can glide on a branch without rustling a leaf," said Pengli. "Your fruit will be in no danger from me."

For a moment Pengli hung upside-down on a branch of the rootomom tree, then, hooking her sharp claws into the bark, she crawled noiselessly out of sight.

"I wonder if Kirak will see us when we leave the forest? Momo, tell me if he's flying overhead," said Benja, as he picked his way through the trees. Momo was perching quietly on the edge of a weaver birds' basket. It was hard for him to be still but he was determined not to shake the rootomom tree.

As they came into the sunlight at the edge of the forest, Benja stopped.

"Look up, Momo. Is Kirak in sight?"

"I see a speck in the sky," said Momo. "Could that be Kirak?"

"It might be," said Benja. "Tell me what happens as we walk along."

"The speck is getting bigger. It's coming lower. I can see it is Kirak."

"Then it's time for the carpenter ants to do their work," said Benja. "Kind ants," he called, "please saw off the leaves around the rootomom fruit."

The ants set to work and a trail of leaves fell about Benja's feet as he followed the path across the plain. Soon the topmost branches of the rootomom tree were bare but the rootomom fruit was still hidden.

"Kirak is hovering over us," said Momo.

"Let's stop here," said Benja. "If we go too close to the village Kirak may be frightened away."

Benja stood still. Rootomom leaves rained down over him as the ants sawed away. Momo jumped down from the basket.

"I can see the orange fruit shining in the sun," he cried excitedly.

"Then it's time for the ants to stop sawing," said Benja. "They must leave enough leaves to hide my friends. Thank you, kind carpenters," he called up to the ants. "You've done enough. Momo, where's Pengli?"

"She's curled on a bare branch beside the rootomom fruit. She looks as if she were dead. Now Kirak's swooping down!" Momo held his breath. "He's aiming at Pengli! He's stretching out his long, bare neck and bending down his ugly bald head! He's going to grab her!"

"No!" cried Benja. "Don't let him take her!"

Momo hopped up and down. "She moved! She moved! Kirak's flying away!"

"What shall I do now? Kirak didn't eat the fruit." Benja's hopes turned to disappointment.

"Wait, Benja! Kirak's coming back. Pengli's playing dead again. Kirak's going to land on the tree! I can see his claws! Pengli twitched her tail! Kirak flew up! Now Pengli's playing dead again. Here comes Kirak! Here comes Kirak! Kirak! Kirak!" Momo chattered in excitement.

"I wish I could see what's happening!" exclaimed Benja. "What's Kirak doing to Pengli?"

"Pengli's safe. She hid in the leaves. Kirak looks angry. He's flying away."

"If only Jara were here! He might know how to bring Kirak back."

"Kirak's *coming* back! He's seen the rootomom fruit. He's diving for it! He's taken it! He's taken it! He's taken it!"

Momo sprang onto Benja's shoulder. All at once the rootomom tree began to shake. A rustling spread through its branches. Out from its leaves came the ants and the popping toads and Pengli.

"You won't need us anymore," they said. "We must go back to the forest. Your tree is too bare to live in. Look how the leaves are falling!"

"There is nowhere to hide," said Momo. "I must leave too." He jumped to the ground.

"My friends," said Benja. "I'll miss you. How can I thank you?"

"Come and visit us in the forest," they chorused, "but heed good advice when it's given and don't be tempted again by the rootomom fruit."

"I know better now," declared Benja. He watched his friends disappear into the shadows. Then he set off for the village. As he walked along, the rest of the rootomom leaves dropped in papery curls to the ground. They rustled and crackled as Benja's bare feet scuffled through them.

Benja's mother heard the strange rustling. She came to the doorway of her hut.

"Benja!" she exclaimed. "The spell's broken! Your tree is dying! Kirak must have swallowed the seed in your rootomom fruit!" She hugged Benja. "You won't need to go to the forest for borra bark for a while. We can burn the wood from your tree as soon as it falls from your head."

"I'll miss my friends from the forest," said Benja.

"I'm still here," said Chakeetoh. He ran down Benja's arm. "If you tuck me inside your shirt I can go wherever you go."

"Then I won't be lonely," said Benja. "I was sad that my other friends left me."

When Benja lay down that night Chakeetoh nestled behind his ear. The bare rootomom branches made strange scratching noises in the dust.

Benja fell asleep thinking about all that had happened to him since he swallowed the rootomom seed. The sun was rising when he woke.

"Good morning, my young friend," said a familiar voice in his ear.

Quickly Benja sat up.

"You couldn't do that yesterday," chuckled Jara. "You couldn't sit up in a hurry."

Benja looked around. There, lying on the ground behind him, was the leafless rootomom tree. He put his hands up to his head. All he could feel was his hair.

"Jara," he cried, "the rootomom tree fell off in the night! I'm myself again! The year and a day has ended!"

"I told you it would," squawked Jara.

"How can I thank you? I wish I could do something for you."

"You can, my young friend," said Jara. "From now until you are an old, old man you can tell the story. You can warn others that it is not wise to be tempted by the fruit of the rootomom tree."

"I'll tell the whole world what happened to me," said Benja.

"The world's a big place, Benja. Start with your own village." Jara spread his wings and flew away.

Benja watched him go. Then he jumped up and down on the lifeless rootomom tree.

"Rootomom tree, soon you'll be burnt to ashes!" he shouted.
Laughing, he ran inside the hut to wake his mother.